Grandmother
Georgia's
Hats

If you enjoy reading this book, you might
also like to try another story
from the MAMMOTH STORYBOOK series:

Grandmother
Georgia's
Hats

Franzeska G. Ewart

Illustrated by **Anni Axworthy**

mammoth

To Gillian

First published in Great Britain in 2000
by Mammoth, an imprint of Egmont Children's Books Limited,
a division of Egmont Holding Limited,
239 Kensington High Street, London W8 6SA

Text copyright © 2000 Franzeska Ewart
Illustrations copyright © 2000 Anni Axworthy

The moral rights of the author and illustrator have been asserted.

The rights of Franzeska Ewart and Anni Axworthy to be
identified as the author and illustrator of this work have been asserted by
them in accordance with the Copyright, Designs and Patents Act 1988

ISBN 0 7497 4230 5

10 9 8 7 6 5 4 3 2 1

A CIP catalogue record for this book
is available from the British Library

Printed in Great Britain
by Cox & Wyman Ltd, Reading, Berkshire

Contents

~

1. The Mexican sunhat

Harry loved going to stay in his Grandmother Georgia's house. He loved the winding staircases and the pictures that Grandmother Georgia had brought back from her travels. He loved the polished wooden floors that echoed to the sound of Grandmother Georgia's feet as she danced, and he loved the tiny roof garden that surprised everyone, right at the top of the narrowest staircase.

But, most of all, Harry loved the stories

1

that Grandmother Georgia told. There was not one thing in the house that didn't have a story inside it. Other people could tell stories: his father, who laughed loudly at his own jokes; his mother, who could make up songs too; and his teacher, who could draw pictures as well. But no one could tell stories like Grandmother Georgia. No one else could pick things up and shake the stories right out of them like Grandmother Georgia could.

On the landing there hung a moose's head. It had always been there, and ever

since Harry was a little boy it had glared down disapprovingly. It had a most unpleasant expression on its face, as though it was about to spit on you. When he was small, Harry had been frightened to go to the bathroom at night because of it. He used to imagine that it would sprout legs and jump down on to his head, and that would be the end of him.

Harry was a big boy of seven now, and knew that the moose's head was full of sawdust and its eyes were made of glass, but it still gave him an uncomfortable feeling.

'Where did it come from, Grandmother?' he would ask.

'From an admirer, Harry,' Grandmother Georgia would say, reaching up to straighten one of the hats which hung from its velvety antlers. 'Someone I knew a long time ago. He was an ostrich farmer, and he was even taller than your daddy is. He wore shiny brown boots and he always carried a gun.

'He gave me it as a token of affection,' she would go on, raising her eyebrows slightly. 'Not really my cup of tea,' she would finish. 'But as they say, Harry, you shouldn't look a gift horse in the mouth.'

The first time Grandmother Georgia had said that, Harry had wrinkled his nose and peered up at the moose's head. It wasn't a horse, he thought. It was a moose. And you couldn't see into its mouth even if you had wanted to. Then Grandmother Georgia had laughed and said, 'It's just an expression, Harry! It means, you shouldn't find fault with a gift.' And she had raised her eyebrows again and sighed. 'He meant well, Harry. And it does make an excellent hatstand.'

Of all the wonderful places Harry visited with Grandmother Georgia, Harry's favourite was the park which was just down the road. They went there almost every day after breakfast.

'Which hat shall I wear today?' Grandmother Georgia would ask. Then they would look up at the hats and Harry would try to avoid eye contact with the moose. He never minded which hat Grandmother Georgia chose, because he knew whichever one it was it would be brimful of stories.

One late spring morning Harry and Grandmother Georgia stood below the moose. 'It's very sunny today, Harry,' Grandmother Georgia said. 'I think I'll wear the sunhat.'

She pulled down a bright red hat with a pattern of blue and orange flowers, pressed it down on to her white curls, and off they went.
'I got this hat in

Mexico, Harry,' she told him, her blue eyes sparkling. 'At a *fiesta*, which is a kind of party with lots of music and dancing.

There were people dancing on their hats!'

Harry looked up in amazement. 'Their *hats*?' he repeated. 'Didn't they get awfully bashed?'

'They certainly did, Harry,' Grandmother Georgia laughed. 'And dusty. But I thought I'd have a go, so I bought this sunhat and I threw it on the ground,' – she took off the sunhat and flung it on to the pavement – 'and I danced round and round its brim with the tiniest of steps.'

Harry hoped that Grandmother Georgia would show him how she had danced with the tiniest of steps and, for a moment, she looked as though she might. But then a woman came round the corner pushing a

pram. She stopped just in
time and gave Grandmother
Georgia a disapproving
look. Grandmother
Georgia picked up
the sunhat, brushed
it down, and put it
back on her head.

'Come along, Harry,' she said quickly.

'What happened then?' Harry asked.

Grandmother Georgia's eyes clouded.
'Well, Harry, the story has a rather unhappy
ending. A herd of bulls with huge horns
came charging down the street and all but
knocked me over. Imagine, Harry – I could
have been gored!' And she hurried through
the park gates and down the grassy slope to
the edge of the pond.

Harry began to throw bread to the ducks. Grandmother Georgia was pointing out a bird that *wasn't* a duck and telling Harry that it was a grebe when suddenly she stopped.

'Look over there, Harry,' she said quietly. 'That isn't a duck either.' She pointed to a big black bird sitting on a buoy, its long neck bent like an 's'. 'It's a cormorant. And look! It's got a chick!'

Harry narrowed his eyes to see the baby cormorant. It was black too, and it had a big white beak that was far too large for its face.

'Do you think its wing's hurt, Grandmother?' Harry said worriedly.

Grandmother Georgia narrowed her eyes too. 'You're right, Harry. I think we ought to catch it. We don't want a fox getting it.' And, without a

moment's hesitation, she pulled off her sunhat
and her Wellingtons and her jeans, and
waded into the pond. When the water
reached her waist she plunged in and
swam, her arms moving like the beaters on
an egg-whisk.

Harry's heart was
in his mouth as
Grandmother
Georgia picked
up the baby
cormorant and
swam back. This
time she turned over and held the chick
against her chest, changing hands with
every stroke. A little crowd had gathered
beside Harry and, as Grandmother
Georgia emerged from the water looking
very cold and streaked with green, they
cheered primly.

The baby cormorant's big black eyes

cried silently up at Harry as he took it gently from Grandmother Georgia. One of its wings hung at an odd angle.

'We must take it to the park keeper right away, Harry,' Grandmother Georgia said, rubbing herself rather uselessly with her jeans and pulling a long strand of pond weed out of her mouth. 'He'll know what to do.'

She pulled her damp clothes on with some difficulty and set off at a run. Harry tried to follow her but the baby cormorant was very unhappy and it began to struggle.

'Grandmother!' Harry called. 'I can't hold it. It's too wet and slippy. Can I put it in your sunhat?'

Grandmother Georgia stopped and frowned down at Harry. 'It will *ruin* it, Harry,' she told him crisply. 'Birds are not toilet-trained, you know.'

'Please, Grandmother,' said Harry. 'It'll feel much safer. It'll think it's in a nest.'

Grandmother Georgia thought about it for a while. Then, with a bigger-than-ever shiver she said, 'Oh very well, Harry. To be honest, that sunhat just reminds me of bulls, which is *not* a happy memory!'

And she took off the hat and held it while Harry laid the baby cormorant inside. As if by magic the chick settled down and looked from Grandmother Georgia to Harry with its sad big eyes.

The park keeper was a large man with a moustache. He smiled at Harry and took the sunhat from him. He examined the baby cormorant gently.

'I know just what to do,' he said at last.

'We thought you would,' said Harry.

'I'll take it to the RSPB,' he said.

'Would you like to borrow the sunhat?' Harry asked politely. 'It's ruined.'

The park keeper smiled. 'It's all right,' he said. 'We have special boxes designed for the purpose.' And he lifted the baby cormorant out and handed the sunhat to Harry. 'It'll wash,' he said.

'No thank you,' said Harry. 'We insist you keep it. It reminds my grandmother of bulls,' he added by way of explanation.

The park keeper laughed. 'It's a lovely hat,' he said, putting it on. 'Does it suit me?'

Harry looked at Grandmother Georgia and then he looked back at the park keeper. The park keeper pressed the hat against his ears and smiled even more.

'Does it?' he asked again.

'Yes,' said Harry quickly.

'Yes,' said Grandmother Georgia.

Harry and Grandmother Georgia ran all the way home. Grandmother Georgia's nose had turned quite blue. Her Wellingtons made a swishing sound as she ran and her curls were flattened against her forehead.

When they got home she ran up the steps two at a time. 'Hot shower,' she said, gritting her teeth to keep them still.

'You know something, Grandmother?' Harry asked, carefully pulling off Grandmother Georgia's left Wellington. There was a slight *splash*.

'What?' Grandmother Georgia asked, mopping up the water with her jumper.

'When I said your sunhat suited the park keeper,' Harry went on, and then he paused.

'Yes?' smiled Grandmother Georgia, wrapping a towel round her head.

'I didn't really mean it,' Harry finished quietly.

Grandmother Georgia laughed very loudly and slammed the bathroom door behind her.

'Neither did I, Harry!' she called over the sound of the hot shower.

2. A wonderfully elegant hat

The next time Harry came to stay with Grandmother Georgia it was summer. There was a dreadful heatwave and when Harry arrived in the afternoon it was too hot even for the roof garden.

'Let's go to the park right now,' said Grandmother Georgia after she had squeezed three lemons into water and added mint leaves. She filled a glass and handed it to Harry. 'We can have a look to see how the cormorant's getting on. I think I spotted

15

the chick last week. It looks fine now.'

Harry drank the lemonade and nodded. The park was exactly where he wanted to go.

'Can I take a jam jar, Grandmother?' he asked. 'Maybe there'll be something to catch.'

Grandmother Georgia hunted around in the cupboard and found one. 'Upstairs and change into something more comfortable, Harry,' she said. 'Then we'll choose my hat and go.'

It took Grandmother Georgia longer than usual to choose a hat from the moose. 'You know, Harry,' she frowned, 'it should really be the sunhat today. I must have something that keeps the sun off my face.' She gave a little tut and studied the hats again, and the moose looked down at her as though it wanted to tut as well.

But at last she said, 'Ah yes. The Paris

number,' and
reached up to
unhook a tiny
black hat from
which there hung
a large piece of
black net studded
with shiny black sequins.

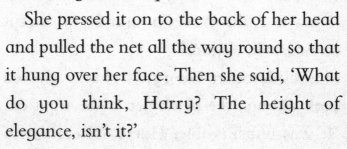

She pressed it on to the back of her head
and pulled the net all the way round so that
it hung over her face. Then she said, 'What
do you think, Harry? The height of
elegance, isn't it?'

Harry looked carefully up at the hat. It
was really hard to think of good answers to
Grandmother Georgia's questions, the
second one of which he hadn't really
understood. Somehow, it just didn't strike
him as the kind of hat for an afternoon in
the park – though he couldn't have
explained why.

'What's "the height of elegance",
Grandmother?' he asked eventually.

'It means, as tasteful as you can possibly
get, Harry!' Grandmother Georgia replied.
She patted the hat and took a few steps,
waving her hips slightly from side to side in a
way Harry had never seen her do before.
'This, Harry, is a designer hat,' she told him.
'I got it at the Paris Fashion Show. Isn't it
wonderfully elegant?'

Grandmother Georgia's cheeks glowed
pink through the black net as she went on.
'It was unbelievable, Harry. There was a
long platform, called a catwalk, and the
models came out wearing the most
incredible clothes.

'They were all taller than your daddy,
with long, long legs. And the clothes were
dotted with diamonds, and hung with
feathers, and encrusted with pearls.'

Harry shut his eyes tight and tried to

imagine them.

'Did the models
wear all sorts of hats,
Grandmother?' he asked.

'Did they ever!' said
Grandmother Georgia.
'Hats with brims as big
as coffee tables! Hats
with half an ostrich
stuck to them! Hats
with ribbons so glossy
you could see your
face in them!'

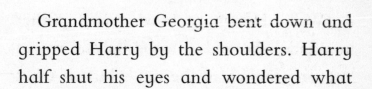

Grandmother Georgia bent down and
gripped Harry by the shoulders. Harry
half shut his eyes and wondered what

19

Grandmother Georgia's view must be like through all those sequins.

'Then I saw it,' she breathed. 'Perched on top of the most elegant model in the whole of Paris – this hat! And I just had to have it, Harry, no matter how much it cost.'

Suddenly Grandmother Georgia stood up and walked towards the door. 'Come along, Harry. I'll tell you the rest of the story as we go.'

The sun was hotter than ever as they walked to the park. The gardens were full of flowers and buzzing with lazy bees. Harry clutched the jar to his chest and trotted along happily.

'Then what happened?' he asked.

Grandmother Georgia took a deep breath.

'Well, Harry, it was really rather romantic,' she said. 'I stood up and waved my programme in the air, which is what

one does at such things,
and a man on the other
side of the catwalk saw
me. He was a very
dashing young man, Harry, with a large
moustache.'

'Like the park keeper,' Harry said.

'No,' said Grandmother Georgia rather
sharply. 'Not at *all* like the park keeper.'

They walked through the gates and
Harry ran on ahead and tumbled down the
slope to the pond's edge. He screwed up his
eyes and looked across to the buoy, and sure
enough there sat the big cormorant, its
wings stretched out on either side.

'It's drying its wings, Harry,' said
Grandmother Georgia. 'And look – see the
baby?'

For a while they said nothing. The young
cormorant, all black and fluffy and untidy,
with a beak that took up most of its

head, bobbed along on the smooth water. The air, full of scents and birdsong, wrapped them around like a great warm blanket.

'Who *was* the dashing young man, Grandmother?' said Harry at last. Grandmother Georgia laughed as she took up the story again.

'Ah, Harry, none other than the designer of all those marvellous clothes! He came round to where I was sitting and gave a little bow, and he said, "Permit me, *Mademoiselle* (that's French for 'Miss'), to present you with a small gift." And he handed me the very hat I had wanted so much!'

Harry looked up, wide eyed, at Grandmother Georgia's face through the net. 'Wow!' he said and then, 'Why did he do that, Grandmother?' he asked.

Grandmother Georgia bent down again

and, so that the ducks wouldn't hear, she put her mouth close to Harry's ear and whispered. 'He said I was the most beautiful woman in Paris, and that he would consider it an *honour* if I would grace one of his hats with my head!'

Harry opened his mouth to say, 'Wow!' again but, as he did, something caught his eye and, instead of 'Wow!' he shouted, 'Sticklebacks!' very loudly, right into Grandmother Georgia's black sequins. Then he dropped to his knees and began to scoop up jarfuls of water, but each time he looked into the jar he gave a little tut of disappointment. 'Oh, Grandmother,' he said at last. 'I can't catch them!'

Grandmother Georgia pulled back the net of the wonderfully elegant hat and knelt beside Harry. Sure enough, the water was swimming with small brown fish, but as soon

as the jar came in their direction they sensed it and, like a slippery brown cloud, darted out of reach.

'You need a net,' said Grandmother Georgia. 'We'll buy one.'

Harry said nothing, but he had a look in his eyes that Grand-  mother Georgia immediately recognised.

'No!' she said, getting up. 'Absolutely not, Harry. On no account.'

'Please, Grandmother . . .' said Harry, reaching up towards the wonderfully elegant hat.

'Have you any idea how much this cost?' said Grandmother Georgia. 'And you could even think of using it to catch sticklebacks?'

Harry sat down and pulled off his sandals and socks. He dangled his feet over the pond edge. In the distance, the cormorant dived and its ripples rolled over the water to kiss his toes. Grandmother Georgia sat down too and together they counted how long it could hold its breath under water.

Then Grandmother Georgia spoke, and as she did she took the wonderfully elegant hat off and slid it across the grass to touch Harry's hand.

'I've had a rethink, Harry,' she said. 'You can use it as a net. The Paris Fashion Show isn't such a great memory anyway.'

Harry picked up the hat and dipped it in the water before Grandmother Georgia would change her mind. Almost immediately the net filled up with sticklebacks

which seemed to find the black sequins very attractive. Harry trawled a couple of times, then emptied his catch into the jar.

'Cool!' he smiled. Then he turned to Grandmother Georgia and said, in a worried voice, 'Why, Grandmother? What happened next?'

'Well,' said Grandmother Georgia, pulling her legs up underneath her and hugging her knees tightly, 'as I was receiving my gift and gracing the hat with my head, one of the other models came rushing along the catwalk with a face like thunder. That's a "very angry" face, Harry,' she explained quickly and Harry nodded.

'It seems *she* had had a notion of the wonderfully elegant hat too, you see,' she went on. 'And *perhaps*, though I wouldn't say this out loud,' she whispered, 'a tiny little notion of the fashion designer too.

'Anyway, we will, as it were, draw a veil

over the next moments, Harry,' Grandmother Georgia said with a note of finality. 'And we won't spoil the day by discussing it further.'

She stood up brightly. 'How about chicken dansak for tea, Harry?'

Harry stood up too. 'With extra coriander?'

'Natch!' said Grandmother Georgia. 'Race you to the gates!'

Harry and Grandmother Georgia ran up the grassy slope so fast that Harry had to hold the jam jar tight to stop the water from spilling.

They ran so fast that they didn't notice that they had left the wonderfully elegant hat lying in a miserable heap by the side of the pond.

And they ran so fast that they even missed the sight of a large man with a moustache, wearing a bright red sunhat with a pattern of orange and blue flowers, picking it up and putting it in his pocket.

3. The Russian fur hat

The trees in the park had turned brown and red and golden next time Harry and Grandmother Georgia went there, because it was autumn.

As usual, they stood below the moose for quite a long time and the moose stared disapprovingly down at them for quite a long time before Grandmother Georgia said, 'Yes – of course! There's been such a nip in the air lately, Harry. I need a really warm hat today. I'll take the fur one.'

And she reached up and unhooked an enormous hat made of pale grey fur. Harry stared up at Grandmother Georgia with interest. It looked, he thought, as though a squirrel had decided to fall asleep on her head.

'Is it *real*, Grandmother?' he asked, and Grandmother Georgia nodded with a frown.

'Yes, Harry. It's real. *Not* that I approve for one minute of killing animals for their coats,' she said with a shiver. 'It's quite barbaric. But this hat was a gift, many years ago and . . .' and she suddenly turned, reached for Harry's hand and, as she propelled him through the door, promised, '. . . I'll tell you the story, Harry, when we get to the park.'

The walk to the park was a very fast one because there really was quite a nip in the air. Every now and then a brown leaf would escape from a tree and float in front of them, daring them to catch it. Grandmother Georgia had once told Harry that if you managed to catch a falling leaf you got a wish. She had told him that, once upon a time, *she* had caught a falling leaf. But she had never told him what her wish had been, and he had never managed to catch a leaf and get a wish of his own.

'I *wish* I could catch a falling leaf,' he said as they reached the park gates and ran down the grassy slope to the pond's edge.

The cormorant, its wings stretched out on either side, pointed its sharp beak into the air and ignored them. Its chick had almost grown into its beak now, and looked much more cormorant-like.

'Will you tell me the story of the fur hat now?' Harry said as they crouched down and began to throw bread for the ducks.

'It happened long ago in Russia, Harry,' Grandmother Georgia began. 'I was invited to a great ball given by a very rich count in honour of his son who was to be married.

'You have never seen such richness, Harry!' she went on, blue eyes burning like sapphire stars against the snow of her hair. 'The hall was as big as your school playing fields, and it had a great domed ceiling painted sky blue. And on the ceiling there were golden angels, and chariots, and clouds, and stars.

And everywhere there hung crystal chandeliers, which are lights with jewels dangling from them so that every light sparkles into a thousand more. It was breathtaking, Harry.'

Harry shut his eyes and tried to picture what a chandelier must look like. It took his breath away.

'Did you dance with the count, Grandmother?' he asked.

'Didn't I just!' Grandmother Georgia laughed. 'He was a magnificent dancer, and a very handsome man. But, charming though he was, Harry, his heart was not in the right place.'

Harry wrinkled up his nose. He looked at his chest, and then he looked down at his knees. He took a quick look under his left arm. At last he said, 'Where *was* his heart, Grandmother?'

Grandmother Georgia laughed again and

hugged him. 'It's just an expression, Harry,' she explained. 'It means he was not really a very nice man. And so, when he asked me to accompany him on his sledge with its six jet-black horses, I was just a little unsure.'

Harry looked up at the fur hat, sitting like a grey squirrel on Grandmother Georgia's head. 'Did *he* give you the hat?' he whispered.

'Yes, Harry. He did,' Grandmother Georgia told him. 'He said he didn't want me catching cold.'

'And you *did* go on his sledge with the six jet-black horses?' Harry asked.

'Yes – of course I did. We all did. There were eight of us, and it was wonderful! We galloped through the forest along a tiny path between the trees, which were heavy with snow. The branches were so low that our heads got covered, but no one minded. It was so magical, Harry, to travel so fast!'

Harry shut his eyes again and tried to picture six jet-black horses galloping under the Russian trees.

'Did you have to hold on to your hat, Grandmother?' he said, and Grandmother Georgia nodded and laughed even louder.

They were very quiet for a while, and Harry threw the last of the bread to the ducks, who gobbled it hungrily. When he looked up he saw that they were not alone.

Standing just a few steps away, and looking at them through sad eyes, was an

old man. He was very thin and very bent, and his clothes were dirty and full of holes. He had a beard, which was almost white. And he had no hair at all on his head.

'Can you spare ten pence for a cup of tea?' the old man said in a rather crackly voice.

Grandmother Georgia reached into her pocket and took out a pound coin. She handed it to the man and said quietly, 'Have a doughnut too.'

The old man said, 'Much obliged,' and turned to go. As he began to disappear slowly up the slope, Harry looked at Grandmother Georgia, and particularly at the grey squirrel nestling on top of her head.

'Grandmother,' he began, but before he

could say another thing, she took off the Russian hat and handed it to him.

'Go on,' she smiled. 'The count wasn't a very nice man. Incredibly rich men sometimes aren't. I don't really need to be reminded of him!'

Harry took the fur hat and ran up the slope after the old man. When he caught up with him he held out the hat.

'My grandmother and I were wondering . . .' he began. The old man looked at the fur hat in amazement.

'For me?' he asked, taking the hat and turning it upside down. Harry hadn't noticed till then that it was lined with red silk, and that there was a big label with a gold crown sewn on to the lining.

'I like that side better,' Harry said. 'Why don't you turn it inside out? It'll be warmer for the winter.'

The old man smiled and pulled the hat so

that the red silk lining spilled out in all its glory. Its colour gleamed and its embroidered crown shone brightly golden. 'Much obliged,' said the old man again, putting the hat on. It was rather big for his face, Harry thought, and rather bright for the park.

'It's ever so warm,' the old man said. 'Doesn't your grandmother want it any more?'

Harry shook his head. 'No,' he said firmly. 'It reminds her of someone whose heart wasn't in the right place.'

The old man nodded. 'There's a few of *them* about,' he said. And he turned and walked slowly up the slope, pausing every so often to stroke his new red hat. Harry went back to Grandmother Georgia who was getting up and brushing the leaves off the back of her jacket.

'Come on, Harry!' she said. 'Let's hurry home for some soup before my head freezes.'

As they jogged along the pavement and rounded the corner of Grandmother Georgia's street, a particularly large golden leaf decided to leave its tree and float down right in front of Harry's nose. Without even trying, he reached out his hand and caught it.

'Wow!' he said. 'I caught a falling leaf, Grandmother.'

'Make a wish, then,' Grandmother Georgia said. 'But don't tell.'

Harry closed his eyes tight. He made his wish as loudly as he could, right inside his head. And when he had made it, he took hold of Grandmother Georgia's hand as tightly as he could and said, 'You'll never guess what I wished for, Grandmother.'

And Grandmother Georgia squeezed Harry's hand back. Then she put one finger of the other hand against her lips and she said, 'Shhhhhhh!' and gave him a big wink.

'I'm sure I never shall,' she smiled.

4. The most special hat of all

The next time Harry went to stay with Grandmother Georgia he wasn't seven any more. His birthday was in December, and so he was eight when he and Grandmother Georgia walked to the park through snow-covered streets.

The moose had looked strangely bare when they had stood below it this time. Its antlers still held a few dull-looking berets and a cone-shaped hat made of straw, but on that winter morning there was very little to choose from.

'Could have done with the Russian fur,' Grandmother Georgia said. But then she smiled and said, 'It's all right though, Harry. Today I know *just* which hat to choose. And it has the most special story of all, which I'll tell you when we get to the park.'

Grandmother Georgia reached up and unhooked a plain black hat with a plain little brim and pulled it down over her white curls. Harry looked very puzzled. It was such an *ordinary* hat, he thought, but he said nothing.

On the way to the park Harry was very quiet. The pavement was deep with snow, but someone had cleared the snow to either side to make a narrow path that two people could just walk along if they didn't mind walking very close together. The sky was grey and looked as though it might have more snow inside it, and the world slept very still underneath its white blanket.

'What's wrong, Harry?' Grandmother Georgia said as they reached the park. 'Cat got your tongue?'

Harry wrinkled up his nose and wiggled his tongue carefully. The cat getting your tongue sounded even worse than looking into the moose's mouth. Then he said, 'Is that just an expression, Grandmother?'

Grandmother Georgia laughed and said, 'Yes, Harry – it's just an expression! It means you haven't been talking much.'

Harry thought for a moment and then

he said slowly, 'You know when I caught the falling leaf, Grandmother? And I made a wish?'

Grandmother Georgia nodded. 'Of course I remember, Harry,' she said.

'Well,' Harry said quietly, 'it didn't come true.'

They walked through the park gates and trudged down the snow-covered slope. When they got to the edge of the pond Harry began to throw bread to the ducks.

'What did you wish?' Grandmother Georgia asked.

The cormorant dived into the water with a dull *plop*, then bobbed on the surface beside its chick. They were the same size, and the only difference now was that the young bird didn't have its mother's bright white throat.

'I wished for a birthday party,' Harry told Grandmother Georgia and, as he did, he could feel the prickle of tears in his eyes. Trying to smile, he added, 'They said it just couldn't be helped, and they gave me lovely presents, and they said I'd get one next year for sure.'

Grandmother Georgia put her arm round Harry's shoulders and gave him a squeeze. 'I'm sure it just couldn't be helped,' she said. 'But I'm sorry all the same.'

Then she straightened up and smiled her sunniest smile and said, 'How about making a snowman, Harry? Come on, let's make a really big one!' and she ran through the trees and out into a clearing where no one except the squirrels had spoiled the smoothness of the snow. Harry followed her.

First they made a snowball. That took longer than it should have done because Grandmother Georgia kept wanting to have snowball fights, but eventually they had a good firm one and they rolled it very carefully so that it grew and grew. The bigger it became, the heavier it was to push, and it made a creaking noise as it moved. When they could roll it no further without falling over, they stopped and stuck snow on to it.

Next they made a smaller snowball for
its head. They had what Grandmother
Georgia called a 'devil of a job' lifting it up
on to the body, but at last they managed it
and they stepped back to admire their work.

'It needs a nose, Harry. And a mouth,'
said Grandmother Georgia.

'And eyes,' added Harry, running off to
pick up sticks and fir cones.

The snowman looked fabulous when it
had its big fir-cone nose and its little fir-cone

eyes and its big stick mouth. Harry looked at it, his head to one side.

'I tell you what it needs, Grandmother,' he said at last, eyeing Grandmother Georgia in the way he often had before. 'It needs a hat!'

This time, though, Grandmother Georgia shook her head very firmly, and she gave Harry a look which he knew meant it was useless to ask again.

'Not *this* hat, Harry,' she said. '*This* hat is much, much more special than the Mexican sunhat, and the wonderfully elegant French hat, and the Russian fur hat. Shall I tell you why, Harry?'

And then Harry suddenly remembered that in the excitement of the snowman he had quite forgotten to ask Grandmother Georgia to tell him the story of the ordinary-looking black hat.

'Oh, Grandmother!' he said. 'It must be a *very* special story. What happened?'

'Well, Harry,' Grandmother Georgia said. 'I bought this hat in an enormous hurry, almost exactly eight years ago. I bought it because it was snowing, and I had come out without a hat, and I was going to a hospital, and I knew I would get my hair very wet without one.'

Harry wrinkled his nose and looked at Grandmother Georgia with a worried expression.

'A hospital, Grandmother? Was somebody ill?'

Grandmother Georgia sat down on a heap of snow left over from the third snowball fight. 'No, Harry – nobody was ill,' she said gently. 'I was going to see your mummy. She had just had a baby – her first baby. *My* first grandson!'

She smiled and picked up a handful of snow, and she let the snow trickle down on to Harry's nose so that he twitched it and laughed.

'Me!' he cried. 'You wore the hat to visit *me*! Is that why it's special?'

'Yes, Harry,' said Grandmother Georgia. 'Of course that makes it my most special hat. It doesn't have any bad memories, you see. *All* it makes me think about are good things.'

She got up and stretched her arms out on either side like a cormorant drying its wings. 'So, you may *not* have it for the snowman. And in fact . . .' she picked up a huge handful of snow and threw it as hard as she could in the direction of the snowman's head, 'the snowman won't be needing a hat when I'm finished with him!'

And as the snowman's head fell off and broke into a dozen pieces, and as Harry ran to make another snowball, three of the strangest people appeared above the brow of the hill. They seemed to walk extremely slowly so that for a while Grandmother Georgia and Harry only saw their heads above the white of the snow.

One head had a big moustache and it was wearing a sunhat with a pattern of blue and orange flowers.

One head was small and rosy-cheeked and it was wearing a wonderfully elegant black hat with a veil studded with black sequins.

And the third head had a big white beard and it was wearing a silky red hat with a bright gold crown embroidered on its front.

'Oh!' said Harry in surprise.

'Oh!' smiled Grandmother Georgia in delight. 'Have you come for Harry's party?'

And the park keeper, and his rosy-cheeked wife, and the old man all nodded as their bodies appeared above the white of the snow. Each one was carrying a little bag, and when they emptied their bags, Harry had a birthday cake, and birthday lemonade, and birthday biscuits, and three little birthday presents to open.

The park keeper and his wife gave him a baseball cap, which they explained had been in Lost Property for over a year and which they assured him had had a good wash. The old man gave him a flat cap which he said had belonged to a friend of his and which Grandmother Georgia said Harry could

wear after it had been to the dry cleaners.
And Grandmother Georgia gave him a
straw hat with a blue and white ribbon,
which she said he could wear next time he
came to stay with her in the spring.

'Now!' Grandmother Georgia said after
Harry had tried on all the hats except the
flat cap, 'Games!' and she turned a
cartwheel just to get them started.

It was the best birthday party Harry had ever had, with some of the best games. The park keeper and his wife and the old man didn't want to run around much, but they were very good at holding their arms out like cormorants for Harry and Grandmother Georgia to run underneath. And of course the party hats were better than anyone could ever have imagined.

When it was time to go home and they had said their thank yous and goodbyes, Harry and Grandmother Georgia walked along the narrow path in the pavement, very close together.

'My wish *did* come true,' Harry said happily.

And Grandmother Georgia, smiling down at him under the brim of the very special black hat, winked and said, 'So did mine, Harry – so did mine!'

If you enjoyed this
MAMMOTH STORYBOOK
look out for

Blair the Winner

Theresa Breslin
Illustrated by *Ken Cox*
~

It's not fair being in the middle,
like Blair.

Little baby Willis is a pest.
Big sister Melissa thinks Blair's the pest.
And all the family never stop nagging!

But it's Blair who saves the day on a
camping trip that goes wrong . . .

If you enjoyed this

look out for

Frankie's House-Tree

Pippa Goodhart
Illustrated by *Leonie Shearing*
~
Frankie's got a living house-tree!

It's a leafy den in the spring . . . Summer
brings flowers, birds and bees . . . In
autumn the golden leaves tumble . . . And
in winter there's a Christmas surprise for
the animals in the garden.